Venus th...
and Further wild sto...

Venus had never seen the moon
before and she couldn't take her eyes
off it . . . When it was full, its beams
poured down through the trees and
sent long dark shadows across the
lawn, bathing the whole world in
peaceful silence. Everything looked
frozen in its cool glow. Even the
tomatoes above Venus's head shone
blue like little moons themselves. She
looked up through the leaves and
knew that no matter what she did she
had to go to the moon.

Twelve wild stories from a garden.

Also by the same author:

Venus the Caterpillar and Further Wild Stories

Colin Thompson

Illustrations by the author

Hodder
Children's
Books

a division of Hodder Headline plc

First published in Great Britain in 1996
by Hodder Children's Books

A Catalogue record for this book is available from the
British Library

ISBN 0340-61996-1

Typeset by Hewer Text Composition Services, Edinburgh.

Printed and bound in Great Britain by Cox & Wyman Ltd,
Reading, Berks.

Hodder Children's Books
A division of Hodder Headline plc
338 Euston Road
London NW1 3BH

Contents

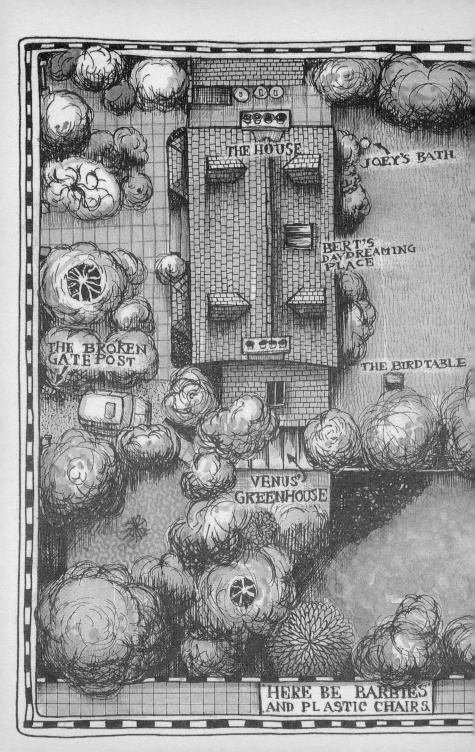

THE HOUSE

JOEY'S BATH

BERT'S
DAYDREAMING
PLACE

THE BROKEN
GATE POST

THE BIRD TABLE

VENUS'
GREENHOUSE

'HERE BE BARBIES'
AND PLASTIC CHAIRS.

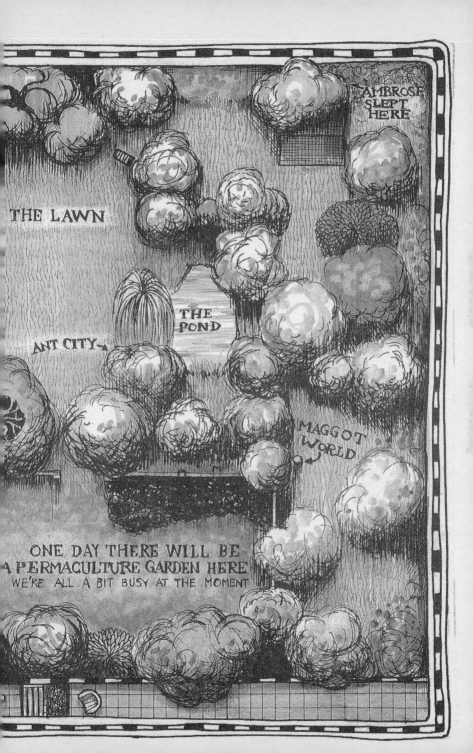

For my grandchildren
Ella, Duncan and Ruth

Christmas

At the end of a quiet street, at the edge of a large town, stood a beautiful old house. On either side in flat silent gardens the other houses sat cold and weary. There was heat inside them made by white boxes on kitchen walls that clicked and moaned through the winter nights, but outside the houses looked dull and lifeless. Their chimneys stood damp and empty above closed up fireplaces.

Only at the house called fourteen was it any different. The garden was like a sleeping jungle. It was the middle of winter. The leaves had fallen and the trees stood dark and quiet but still the garden was full of life. Birds cluttered up the branches and small secret creatures tunnelled through the thick piles of leaves hunting for food.

The house itself looked warm and comfortable like a big armchair. There was no white box on its kitchen wall and in its fireplaces real fires danced and crackled. Every single brick was warm and cosy. The whole house seemed to glow in the November darkness.

The days of winter moved slowly on and it started to get very cold. The sun kept low all day. Its light was weak and tired, and gave out so little heat that the heavy frost lay undisturbed from dawn to dusk. Every twig, every blade of grass, was covered in crystals of ice that sparkled like a million tiny diamonds as the thin sun danced through them. A deep cold crept into every corner. In the deserted factories across the canal, ferns of ice crystals covered the windows and from the pale roofs icicles hung down towards the freezing ground. The canal itself froze over, dark dull grey at first then white as frost covered the surface. Ducks flew in, sprawling and sliding across the ice, trailing wild skid marks and frantic footprints as they tried to slow down.

As the swans came down they crashed into each other and sent the ducks scattering in all directions. For weeks the canal was covered with irritable clumsy birds falling down at every step yet too confused to fly away to warmer waters.

As the winter sunk deeper and deeper into the earth so the worms and moles dug down below it. Sensible animals had flown away to warmer lands while those that were left behind did the best they could to survive. Some crept into their beds and hibernated. Others fluffed themselves up and waited for spring. People, unable to adapt like most animals, hid in thick clothes and blew clouds of steam into the air.

In December even the clouds grew cold and slipped quietly away. For two weeks the sky was pale blue from side to side. It was a thin wintery sky that seemed much less part of the world than the bright skies of summer. Far above, in its highest reaches, the smoke lines of aeroplanes crossed from one horizon to another, covering the world in white cobwebs.

Dennis the owl sat in his big oak tree and shivered.

'I wish I could hibernate,' he said.

'Well, why don't you?' asked a robin, sitting on a branch above him.

'I've tried,' said Dennis, 'but I keep falling asleep.'

'Yes, but . . .' the robin started to explain but Dennis wasn't listening. He was looking up at the sky. The sun had given up and gone off to Australia, and thick black clouds were rolling across the town. It was as if someone was wrapping the world up in a heavy eiderdown. It was only midday but it had grown so dark that it felt like evening.

'Oh well,' said Dennis, 'time for bed.'

'Don't be silly,' said the robin. 'It's only midday.'

'But it's dark,' said Dennis, 'it must be bedtime.'

'It isn't always bedtime just because it's dark,' said the robin.

'Of course it is,' said Dennis.

'What about thunderstorms?' asked the robin. 'The sky gets really dark when there's a thunderstorm. What do you do then?'

'Go to bed,' said Dennis, and then he added, 'What do you do?'

'Hide under a branch until it's finished,' said the robin. 'And get wet.'

'That's clever,' said Dennis and went to bed.

Two days before Christmas it snowed. The wind stopped blowing, the bitter cold air seemed to grow warmer and at midnight the snow began to fall. The big white flakes floated down from the clouds in total silence. Other sounds grew fainter too. As the snow settled on the roads, the noise of the traffic grew softer. The whole city faded to a quiet murmur, quieter than the countryside. And beyond the city the countryside itself was as silent as an empty dream.

In the garden the animals that lived by night awoke to find their homes buried. The rabbits and the mice made new tunnels through the snow. Even though it was the first snow that many of them had seen, they knew by instinct what to do. Only Dennis the Owl was confused. He hopped out of his hole in the oak tree and stood on the branch.

'Where's all the colour gone?' he said. 'It's washed away.'

Apart from the yellow squares of light from the windows across the lawn everything was white. Dennis walked along where he thought the branch should be and fell off. He floundered around on the ground kicking and flapping great clouds of snow into the air until he finally shook himself free and fluttered back up to the tree.

'Help, I'm on fire,' he shouted. 'There's smoke everywhere.' But it was just the snow.

As daylight appeared the wind began to grow. The snow that had fallen as softly as feathers now began to dance in frantic circles. It grew until it was a blizzard running round and round the houses in a silent frenzy. It clung to walls and windows and piled itself up in great drifts against doors. Every animal fluffed itself up against the cold and waited. Birds sat huddled under branches while rabbits and mice peered out from their tunnels and watched nature's fury. It raged for hours until the whole world was painted white.

Inside the houses people slept. The snow on the windows blocked out the daylight so that all morning it was as dark as early dawn. Those who did wake up at the right time found it impossible to tell what time of day it was and others, waking late, looked at their watches in disbelief. Most of them, finding they were late for work, took the day off and went back to bed. The people who did try and travel found they couldn't get anywhere. The trains were frozen to the tracks; the buses locked up and cold and their cars wouldn't start. Nature gave the world a day off and as it was nearly Christmas no one really minded.

At the house called fourteen, the two children who lived there went out into the back garden and built a snowman. From inside his tree Dennis the Owl watched wide-eyed as it grew taller and taller on the lawn.

'It'll end in tears,' he said, 'and they'll probably be mine.'

'For goodness sake, Dennis, stop twittering and go to sleep,' said Audrey the Owl.

'But there's a huge giant on the lawn,' said Dennis.

Ethel the chicken stood in the doorway of the hen hut and looked out at the garden. She fluffed out her feathers and settled down in the straw. Sparrows were fluttering from branch to branch sending little gusts of snow tumbling down. The children had cleared the bird table and it seemed as if every bird for miles around was feeding there. The blue tits were fighting round the wire cages of peanuts, and in the trampled snow below clumsy pigeons were pecking up their crumbs.

At lunchtime the man came out and hung a long line of brightly coloured lights across the bushes along the back of the house. Red, blue, green and yellow, at night they glowed in the darkness like big gentle eyes. Dennis thought it was the most beautiful thing he had ever seen.

'It looks like heaven has come down into the garden,' he said.

That night it snowed again, not great wild storms but just enough to fill in the footprints and smooth over the edges so that when everyone woke up on Christmas morning the world was new again. The snowman looked as if he had been wrapped up in a big flowing blanket. The roads that had become grey with traffic were clean and white again. The trees that had shrugged off their coats were covered once more and even the wires between the coloured lights had narrow snow-drifts balanced on them. It had frozen hard during the night and the pools of water where the sun had melted the snow the day before were now frozen through.

It was the first time in sixteen years that there had been snow on Christmas day. Of all the animals in the garden only Ethel was old enough to remember the last time. The two children hadn't even been born then and would probably have children of their own by the time it happened again. And even though the snow began to melt that afternoon, for the family at the house called fourteen it was the best Christmas they had ever known.

Winter Morning

In the dark before dawn
When the moon's crept away,
While the world is still sleeping,
Comes the first breath of day.

From beyond the horizon
Through the tall empty trees
The line of the sunshine
Drifts in with the breeze.

Shining light into windows
A ribbon of gold
Dances over the frost
Of a night grown old.

Then life wakes and stretches,
Crawls into the light,
Drawn out by old instincts
And the famine of night.

The frost beats the sun
And that's how it stays
And we'd rather be sleeping
Through Winter's cold days.

Four Pigeons

Steve and Raymond the pigeons sat on the gutter at the back of the house looking down into the garden. As they watched, a woman came out of the house and tipped some food onto the bird table. As soon as she turned away a crowd of sparrows and starlings flew down from the trees and began fighting and squabbling over the food. The noise was terrific with birds flapping and shouting at each other, pushing and shoving and swearing for all they were worth. Hardly had a bird got a single mouthful before it was being attacked by another.

'See that down there,' said Steve.

'What?' asked his brother Raymond. Steve wasn't actually sure if Raymond was his brother or just another pigeon, but he thought they probably were brothers because they looked so alike. Raymond thought the opposite.

'That food,' said Steve.

'You're thick, you are,' said Raymond, for no

apparent reason.

'Well, if I'm thick,' said Steve, 'then you're thicker.'

'Am not,' said Raymond.

'Are too,' said Steve.

'Not,' said Raymond.

'Are,' said Steve.

'Not.'

Steve did nothing for a bit and then threw himself at Raymond who fell off the gutter. The two birds flapped and crashed at each other until they landed on the bird table scaring all the other birds away.

'Look at all this food,' said Steve and started pecking away at a large currant bun with green mould on the edges.

'You're fat, you are,' said Raymond.

'Well, if I'm fat,' said Steve, 'then you're fatter.'

'Am not,' said Raymond.

'Are too,' said Steve.

'Not,' said Raymond.

'Are,' said Steve.

'Not.'

Steve pecked at his bun for a bit and then threw himself at Raymond who fell off the bird table. The two birds flapped and fought until they ended up in the bushes. The sparrows and starlings, who had flown off when the pigeons had come crashing down, went back to their own battle on the table and carried on with their breakfast.

The two pigeons fluttered out of the bush and sat on a branch getting their breath back.

'You're unhealthy, you are,' said Raymond, between taking deep breaths.

'Well, if I'm unhealthy,' puffed Steve, 'then you're unhealthier.'

'Am not,' said Raymond.

'Are too,' said Steve.

'Not,' said Raymond.

'Are,' said Steve.

'Not.'

Steve said nothing for a bit and then threw himself at Raymond who fell off the branch. The two birds fluttered at each other in the grass but they were so exhausted by now that they could hardly hop off the ground.

17

'Do you ever get the feeling that this has all happened before?' asked Raymond.

'No,' said Steve.

'Well, neither do I then,' said Raymond.

'I bet you do,' said Steve.

'Don't.'

'Well, why did you say it then?' asked Steve.

'Er, because I thought you did,' said Raymond.

'Well, I don't,' said Steve.

Raymond crept under a twig and fluffed up his feathers. He shut his eyes and thought about sleeping. Steve stood and watched him and wondered how they could be so different. He was slim and clever while Raymond was fat and stupid. He was cool and handsome while Raymond was angry and ugly. It was amazing how unlike two brothers could be.

Raymond wondered how two pigeons could be so different. He was clever and slim while Steve was stupid and fat. He was handsome and cool while Steve was ugly and angry. It was obvious that there was no way they could be brothers.

'What was your mother called?' he asked.

'Mum,' said Steve.

'Liar,' said Raymond, 'that's what my mother was called.'

'Well, we're brothers,' said Steve. 'We've got the same mother.'

'Don't be ridiculous,' said Raymond, 'look how different you are from me.'

'Well, if I'm different,' said Steve, 'then you're differenter.'

'Am not,' said Raymond.

'Are too,' said Steve.

'Not,' said Raymond.

'Are,' said Steve.

'Not.'

Steve said nothing for a bit and then fell over.

Rebecca and Liz the pigeons sat on the gutter at the back of the house looking down into the garden. There were two other pigeons fighting on the lawn. They puffed out their chests and flapped at each other like a couple of over-stuffed cushions.

'See that down there,' said Rebecca.

'What?' asked Liz.

'Those two idiots down there,' said Rebecca.

'How long have you had that bald patch?' asked Liz.

'What bald patch?' asked Rebecca. 'I haven't got a bald patch.'

'Yes, you have,' said Liz, 'on the back of your head.'

'Well, if I'm bald,' said Rebecca, 'then you're balder.'

'Am not,' said Liz.

'Are too,' said Rebecca.

'Not,' said Liz.

'Are,' said Rebecca.

'Not.'

Rebecca said nothing for a bit and then threw herself at Liz who fell off the gutter. The two birds flapped and crashed at each other until they landed on the bird table, scaring all the other birds away.

'Look at all this food,' said Rebecca and started pecking away at a brown potato.

'You're fat, you are,' said Liz.

'I know,' said Rebecca, 'I'm much fatter than you.'

'Are not,' said Liz.

'Am too,' said Rebecca.

'Not,' said Liz.

'Am,' said Rebecca.

'Not.'

Rebecca pecked at her potato for a bit and then threw herself at Liz who fell off the bird table. The two birds flapped and fought until they ended up in the bushes. The sparrows and starlings, who had flown off when the pigeons had come crashing down, went back to their own battle on the table and carried on with their breakfast.

The two pigeons fluttered out of the bush and sat on a branch getting their breath back.

'Hey, girls,' said Raymond, 'come on now. You're behaving like a couple of kids.'

'Yeah,' said Steve, 'that's no way for ladies to carry on.'

'What!' exclaimed Rebecca. 'And what do you two think you've been doing for the last half an hour?'

'What are you talking about?' asked Raymond.

'You two,' said Liz. 'You've been at it like a couple of stupid kids.'

'Have not,' said Steve.

'Have too,' said Liz.

'Have not,' said Raymond.

'Have,' said Rebecca.

'Not.'

Liz and Rebecca said nothing for a bit and then threw themselves at Raymond and Steve. The four birds jumped at each other, puffing themselves up as big as they could and calling each other every rude name they could think of. Rabbits covered their children's ears as they hurried by and ants ran for their lives. Feathers flew everywhere until at last the four birds stood exhausted and panting in a circle of trampled grass.

'Let that be a lesson to you,' said Steve.

'Yeah,' said Raymond, 'just you watch it or we'll sort you out again.'

'*You* sort *us* out,' laughed Liz. 'Get real.'

'Come on, girls,' said Steve, 'be honest, we won.'

'Yeah,' said Raymond, 'we let you off because you're girls.'

'You're unbelievable,' said Liz.

'Well, if we're unbelievable,' said Steve, 'then you're unbelievabler.'

'No such word,' said Rebecca.

'Is too,' said Steve.

'Isn't,' said Raymond.

'Is,' said Liz.

'Not.'

Steve and Raymond said nothing for a bit and fell over again. When they got up Rebecca and Liz had gone.

'Women, eh?' said Steve.

'Yeah,' said Raymond.

'Yeah.'

'Still, I thought the bald one was pretty,' said Raymond.

'Not as pretty as the other one,' said Steve.

'Was too,' said Raymond.

'Was not.'

'Was . . .'

Rosie

In the middle of nowhere it was as black as night. Rosie the puppy curled up into a pathetic little ball and tried to sleep. She was very cold and it was a long time since she had had anything to eat, and all around her wild animals roared. Their noise was so loud that the ground shook beneath her. Rosie shook too not just from the cold but because for the first time in her short life she was completely terrified and alone.

She nuzzled around in the tiny darkness but there was no one there. Her brother and sisters and even her mother had all gone. She knew they wouldn't be there. She could still remember what had happened. One by one the others had been taken away until she had been the only one left. She had missed them terribly, missed the loving feel of them all rolling round together in the warm blanket; but then she had had her mother all to herself and for a few days it had been wonderful.

Rosie had been the smallest and the last to go. Someone had picked her up and suddenly it had all gone dark. That's how it was now, dark and alone. She had called out over and over again but no one had come.

The animals roared louder and high above them a terrible, loud crash rolled across the world and it started to rain. A dull flash tried to light the darkness but the thunder chased it away. Rosie hid her face in her paws and shivered and the rain soaked through her fur, and very close in the night one great animal stopped and growled.

Across the motorway the rain came down in great thick curtains. The thunder was so loud that even inside the car with the engine racing they could hear it. Lightning flashed in brilliant sheets, lighting up the world so brightly that for a second the car's headlights were invisible. The red lights of other cars sparkled and flickered in the rain like distant fires.

The woman slowed down and pulled across to the inside lane and as she did so, the car slid sideways like a horse with a broken leg.

'What's the matter?' asked the girl from the back seat.

The woman pulled over onto the hard shoulder and stopped.

'I think we've got a puncture,' she said. They sat in the car as if by waiting everything would be alright. The engine ticked over so softly that in the storm no one could hear it. Only the windscreen wipers moved, waving backwards and forwards in a frantic attempt to clear away the rain. Cars and lorries crawled by, their tail lights winking at them as they slipped away into the darkness.

'I'm not going out in that,' said the woman. 'We'll wait for a bit, it's bound to ease off soon.' So they sat and waited and listened to the radio and outside a few inches from the flat tyre Rosie the puppy, tied up in a sack, grew weaker and weaker.

'Shall I go and have a look?' said the boy. 'See if we have got a puncture?'

'OK,' said the woman.

The boy pulled his collar up and climbed out into the rain. The storm was moving away but it was still raining hard. He walked round the car looking at the wheels, then he climbed back in.

'It's the one at the front on the left,' he said.

When the rain had faded into a soft drizzle the woman and the boy got out and changed the wheel. Rosie had stopped moving. She was now no more than a wet rag like the sack she was imprisoned in. The boy stepped back and stood on the sack, barely a couple of inches from the tiny dog, but he never saw her. They put the flat wheel in the back of the car and the woman got into the driving seat. It was only then, when the boy looked round for something to wipe his hands on, that he noticed the sack. He squatted down and cleaned his fingers, and when he picked the sack up to throw it into the bushes, it moved.

'Come on, get back in the car,' said the woman, but the boy was on the ground pulling at the string.

'There's something here,' he said, 'in this sack.'

'Leave it alone,' said the woman. 'It could be anything.'

'But it's moving,' said the boy. 'It's something alive.'

The woman got out of the car and took the sack from the boy. She undid the string and lifted out the small wet dog. It lay still and pathetic in her hands, no larger than a kitten.

'I think it's dead,' she said, and inside her a giant anger brought tears to her eyes. She held the dead thing against her chest and stood there in the car's headlights as the rain began to fall heavily again. The tears poured down her face into the rain and washed away across the road. She looked up into the sky, up into the storm, and shouted at the top of her voice with a great wild desperate cry of fury. The boy took his mother's hand but there was nothing he could say. His mother's roar had said it all.

"We'll take it home and bury it in the garden,' the woman said. 'It's the least we can do.'

The boy took the tiny animal and put it inside his coat and they drove home in silence. The rain kept falling inside the car as badly as it was outside. The woman could hardly see to drive for her tears and on the back seat the two children sat sad and still. From time to time the woman cursed under her breath but apart from that none of them said a word until they were almost home.

It was past midnight when they left the motorway. Most people were in their beds and the streets were as empty as their hearts. The rain stopped and the clouds moved on, leaving a dark clear sky, and inside the boy's coat the pitiful corpse grew warm, and right outside their house it shook and shivered and the boy cried out and the woman turned round and drove the car right into the gatepost – but it didn't matter.

Even the next morning, when Rosie was warm and dry and drinking milk and sleeping inside the boy's shirt, and they all went out and looked at the broken car, even then it didn't really matter. They mended the car but they left the gatepost to remind them of what had happened. They knew that whoever had been cruel enough to desert Rosie by the roadside had also thrown away all the years of happiness she had to give, happiness that she would now give to them.

Ambrose the Cuckoo

Ambrose the Cuckoo staggered about on the shed roof and tried to wake up. He'd just flown in from Africa and he was exhausted. As usual, he'd got lost and had ended up going the long way round. His head was buzzing, he was starving hungry and his wings were aching. He wasn't sure where he was or where he'd even come from. It might not have been Africa at all, it might have been Turkey or Mexico or none of those places. Wherever it was, it had been hot, very hot, and now it was cold. And wherever it was, there had been cockroaches the size of rabbits, great big juicy delicious insects with soft succulent insides that were a meal all on their own. Now all there were were miserable worms and flies that moved too fast to catch.

It was the same every year. Some idiot would say: 'Hey guys let's take a trip,' and like complete nitwits they did. They never learnt. It was great where they lived. The weather was always warm. It was true there was a lot of sand, hundreds of miles of it to be honest; but there was always plenty to eat, big fat locusts by the million. It was always the same. As soon as they started flying North it began raining. If that wasn't bad enough, in some countries people tried to shoot them. It was always cold and there was never enough to eat. And to make things worse Ambrose was always the last to arrive and all the best nests had already gone.

'Oh man,' said Ambrose, 'this cold is so uncool.' He hunched up his shoulders on the wet roof and shivered.

'It's the last time,' he said. 'Next year I'm staying at home.'

Another cuckoo landed on the shed and slid down the roof towards him. It was his wife Lola and she looked fed up; but then she always looked fed up. Ambrose was not happy. Everything was so uncool.

'Three weeks I've been here,' said Lola. 'Three weeks waiting for Mr Cool to get here.'

'Oh man, just relax,' said Ambrose sliding slowly down the roof. He slid slowly into the gutter, got his feet all tangled up in rotten wet leaves and then toppled gently over the edge into a bush.

'Far out,' Ambrose thought, as he slipped down through the branches. 'Time for bed.'

And he fell fast asleep. He didn't dream. He was too lazy to dream. He just lay on his back under the bush and snored, a weird noise that only a bird that says 'cuckoo' could make. Lola flew down and shouted at him but she knew that once Ambrose was asleep nothing would wake him.

'Great useless uncool lump,' she said and flew off to look for a nest.

It was the time of year when everyone was making or looking for nests. The garden had woken from a long winter. It had shivered through the early days of spring and now the promise of summer filled the air. New leaves flashed brilliant green, the grass began to grow, everyone woke up, and the birds that had been silent for months began to sing. Old visitors like the cuckoos and the swallows, that had spent the winter in warmer places, were drifting back, and inside the house the humans were spring cleaning.

The blue tits were clearing out last year's grass and moss, pulling it to bits and throwing it out. On the ground beneath them, mice were picking it up and using it for their nests. In the treetops pigeons and crows were pushing and poking fresh twigs into their old homes, and inside the twigs themselves small insects were settling down to raise families.

Under the old garden shed the hedgehogs were waking up. They stretched and yawned and snuggled down into their beds of old newspapers. They knew it was time to get up, but when you've been asleep for three months it takes a bit of time to wake up properly. Some of the young hedgehogs had been up and about for a week or more but the old ones were less keen to emerge.

Lola flew from tree to tree looking for the best place to lay her eggs. The pigeons and crows were too big and clumsy, they would just squash her eggs against their lumpy wooden nests. The blue tits were too clever, they built their nests in holes that were far too small for Lola to get in.

Lola flew on round the garden looking for a nest. There were no vacancies in the sparrows' nests. They'd either been taken already or their eggs had hatched. It was the same with the robin and the blackbirds. It happened like this every year. Ambrose was so lazy that everything was always left to the last minute. There was a wren's nest in one of the bushes but it was far too small and the starlings had built theirs in narrow gaps and holes.

The old chicken that had been there every year for as long as Lola could remember was ambling around through the undergrowth. She looked old and clumsy now but she had been in the garden longer than anyone.

'She should know where all the nests are,' thought Lola. 'She must know every inch of the garden like the back of her foot.'

She flew down to talk to her.

'Well,' said Ethel when Lola asked her, 'I suppose you could borrow a bit of my nest.'

'Would *you* sit on one of my eggs for me?' asked Lola.

'I'll sit on anything, dear,' said Ethel. 'At my age you can't afford to be fussy.'

It wasn't much of a choice but it was the only one Lola had. Ethel took her into the hen house and pointed at her nesting box. It was disgusting, it looked as if it hadn't been made for a week and there were bits of old sweaters and envelopes sticking out of the straw. A family of mice were living under one corner of it and there was a red hot-water bottle with a hole in it shoved down the back. And as for the smell, it was like something very old that had been left in a dark damp corner for a very long time. Which is exactly what it was.

'Is that it?' she asked.

'Yes,' said Ethel proudly. 'Lovely isn't it?'

'It's not exactly what I dreamt of,' said Lola.

'Please yourself,' said Ethel, starting to go back

out into the garden.

'No, no,' said Lola, gritting her beak. 'It's lovely.' And closing her eyes and holding her breath she hopped into Ethel's nest and laid an egg.

'Bit small isn't it?' said Ethel. 'But it's a nice colour.'

The old chicken climbed up into the mess of straw and paper and shuffled around until Lola's egg was buried deep in her chest feathers. She closed her eyes and sat clucking softly to herself. Soon she was snoring gently, far away in a land of dreams. Lola tiptoed to the door and flew away as quickly as she could.

The next morning when the children came down from the house to collect the eggs that Ethel's children had laid, they saw the old hen asleep in her nesting box and thought she was ill. She woke up when they spoke to her and when they offered her corn, she got up all stiff legged and clambered out onto the floor.

'Hey, look, she's laid an egg,' said the boy.

'Small isn't it?' said the girl.

'It's big enough for a tiny omelette,' said the boy and they put it in the basket with the other eggs.

Ethel ate her corn and went back to her nest for a nap. She was so old that she couldn't remember things like she'd used to and she didn't notice the egg had gone. She was alright with things that had happened a long time ago. They were just a bit fuzzy round the edges, but what had happened yesterday was different. When she tried to think about that she just ended up daydreaming.

After lunch Lola flew into the hut to see how things were going. She landed in front of Ethel and said, 'How's the egg?'

'Egg,' said Ethel, 'what egg?'

'My egg,' said Lola, 'the one I laid in your nest yesterday.'

'Oh, that egg,' said Ethel. 'What was it called?'

'Called?' said Lola. 'It wasn't called anything. You can't call them anything until they hatch out. You can't give them a name until you know if they're girls or boys.'

'The children did,' said Ethel. 'They gave it a name.'

'What name?' asked Lola. 'What children?'

'The children who come and feed me,' said Ethel. 'They gave the egg a name.'

'OK, OK, what did they call it?' sighed Lola. She knew something had happened to her egg. This was the price you paid for not having to build your own nest. Sometimes things just went wrong, and you had to start all over again.

'They called it Omelette,' said Ethel. 'Lovely name isn't it?'

'Wake up, you great useless lump,' shouted Lola. Ambrose rolled over onto his side, blinked and slowly stood up. His feathers stood out at all angles, his claws were full of mud and his whole appearance made him look as if he had been pulled through a bush backwards, which is exactly what had happened.

'I'll have a large stick insect, man, and make it snappy,' he said. Lola shouted at him some more until at last he was as awake as he was ever going to be.

'Hey, man,' he said with a stupid grin, 'how's it going?'

'Stop calling me man,' said Lola, 'and concentrate.'

'Cool,' said Ambrose, staring at his feet and sulking.

Lola told him what had happened, how she'd been all over the garden looking for a nest, and what had become of the egg she'd left with Ethel.

'It's getting very late,' she went on, 'and you've got to help me find a nest.'

'Far out, man,' said Ambrose.

'Never mind all that,' said Lola. 'You're useless in the air so you look on the ground while I check round all the bushes and trees.'

'Yeah, man,' said Ambrose, 'I'll groove around in the grass.'

'Go on then,' said Lola, 'wipe that stupid grin off your face and get going.'

Ambrose ambled off towards the pond.

'And don't spend hours talking to your reflection,' Lola shouted after him when she saw where he was going.

Ambrose stared into the water and there was his beautiful reflection looking up at him. He was the handsomest bird he'd ever seen, so sleek, so colourful and above all, so cool.

'Hi there, handsome,' he said to himself. His reflection just sat there staring back at him with its eyes full of admiration.

'Ok,' Ambrose thought, 'he's too cool to speak to me, but I can tell he thinks I'm cool too.'

'Will you shut up,' said a voice. 'Some of us are trying to lay eggs and all your useless chattering is putting us off.'

Ambrose looked up and there was an angry moorhen. She swam backwards and forwards in front of him making his beautiful reflection go all wobbly. And half-hidden in the long grass on the other side of the pond was her nest. It was wide and soft and had three eggs in it. It was perfect.

'Oh wow,' thought Ambrose and flew up into the trees to find Lola. He couldn't believe that he'd actually done something clever and useful. Neither could Lola. It took Ambrose a long time to persuade her to go and look at the moorhen's nest but as soon as she did, she was delighted.

'Oh man,' she said, 'I take back all those nasty things I said about you. You're brilliant.'

So while Ambrose distracted the moorhen by singing to his shadow, Lola laid a big beautiful egg in its nest.

As the days passed Lola and Ambrose hid in the treetops above the pond and kept an eye on things. Eventually her beautiful baby hatched out and while the moorhens' backs were turned it rolled the other eggs out of the nest into the water.

'Oh, look at him,' said Lola, 'he's so handsome, just like you.'

'Yeah, cool,' said Ambrose.

'He's grown so fast,' said Lola.

A few weeks later Ambrose and Lola set off back to Africa.

'If we go now,' said Lola, 'we'll miss the rush.'

For once Ambrose didn't argue with her. He missed the hot sunshine and giant cockroaches.

'What about our son?' he asked, but already he could see the endless African plains stretching out in his imagination.

'Oh, he'll be alright,' said Lola. 'He'll catch us up.'

And she was right. Their son was almost ready to follow them. The day after they left, when the moorhen swam away from her nest the baby cuckoo followed her. He raised his tiny head to the sky, opened his bright red mouth and said, 'Cuckoooo . . . splutter . . . glug, glug, glug.'

Ffiona the Shrew

Ffiona the shrew was nervous. Not for any special reason, but because she was a shrew and shrews are always nervous. From the very second they are born to the day they die they are nervous. That's what being a shrew is all about, from the minute they wake up, until they fall asleep at night they are nervous. And even then it doesn't stop, because in their dreams they are nervous too. Other animals, and people too, do wild and wonderful things in their dreams, but not shrews. They just dream about more ways of being scared.

'Not that I dream very often,' said Ffiona.

'Why not?' asked her sister Jjoice.

'I'm too nervous,' said Ffiona.

'What, too nervous to dream?' asked Jjoice.

'No, too nervous to go to sleep,' said Ffiona.

'Well, we're all nervous, dear,' said her brother Ssamson, 'that's what being a shrew is all about.'

'Well, it's hardly surprising,' said Ffiona. 'I mean, well I mean, look at all the awful things there are in the world.'

'Like what?' said Ssamson.

'All the noise, all that stuff,' said Ffiona. 'All the roar of the grass growing and the flowers opening.'

'My goodness,' said the other shrews, 'you really are nervous.'

'Even more nervous than my Uncle Nernernor-norman,' said Jjoice, 'and he was frightened of his own fur. He thought it would grow so long while he was asleep, that it would suffocate him.'

'He was quite right,' said Ffiona. 'You have to be careful how you curl up too, or else your tail might strangle you.'

'Oh, come on,' said Bbasil, 'get real.'

Bbasil wasn't like the other shrews. By comparison to them he was brave and fearless. Bbasil had been to the end of the garden, and he had been inside a paper bag with his eyes open. Bbasil was a legend among shrews and naturally all the others were nervous of him. Bbasil was so brave he was even thinking of calling himself Basil.

'It's true,' said Ffiona. 'My aunt Daisy was killed by her own claws. She fell asleep somewhere too warm and they grew so fast they stabbed her to death before she could wake up.'

'Rubbish,' said Bbasil.

'It's not. It's true,' said Ffiona. 'My mum told . . . oh, oh, what's that?' Ffiona ran into the darkest corner of the tunnel and hid her eyes.

'What?'

'That terrible roaring noise,' said Ffiona. 'It's a dreadful monster coming to get us.'

'No,' said Bbasil. 'It's someone in the house flushing the toilet.'

'Oh, oh, the toilet's coming to get us,' cried Ffiona. 'We're all going to die.'

It was the same every day; there was always something menacing going on. If it wasn't huge noisy leaves crashing down onto the lawn, it was some butterfly flapping its wings together in a threatening way. Ffiona couldn't understand how they survived at all with everything and everyone in the world trying to get them the whole time. When it snowed she thought they'd all be suffocated. When it rained she thought they'd all be drowned and when the sun came out she thought they'd all be cooked.

'It didn't used to be like this,' she said. 'Two weeks ago, when I was young, it was peaceful and safe. It's this terrible modern world we live in.'

'That's not true,' said Ssamson. 'I've been

frightened from the minute I was born.'

'Yes, you're right,' said Ffiona. 'So have I. I was just too scared to remember it.'

'Well I'm not frightened of anything,' said Bbasil and to prove it he closed his eyes.

'Don't do that,' said Ffiona. 'It's terrifying.'

'Oh yeah, well I'm not scared at all,' said Bbasil and he walked straight into the wall.

He wasn't scared but he was incredibly stupid. With his ears ringing, he staggered along the tunnel and out into the daylight. The bright sun hit his face and dazzled him. He walked round and round in circles until he tripped over a pebble and fell straight down a deep drain.

Later on when she heard the news Ffiona would have said, if she hadn't been too scared to, that maybe being scared wasn't such a bad thing after all.

'After all,' said Jjoice, 'if Bbasil had been scared he'd still be here today.'

And she was right because the other shrews led full, happy and terrified lives and all lived to the ripe old age of four weeks.

Joey the Budgerigar

Joey the budgerigar sat on the top of the open window and looked out into the sunshine. Behind him an anxious human voice told him to sit perfectly still, but in front of him a stronger voice coaxed him out into a world he had never known.

'*Joey, good boy, there's a good boy,*' said the human voice. '*Sit still for mummy.*'

'Joey, come on,' said the voice inside his head. 'Fly away.'

The warm sun shone on his soft blue chest. The air smelled sweet and thick with the flowers of summer. Behind him the frightened voice of the woman who had loved him for as long as he could remember, talked softly to him. There were tears in her voice but the call of freedom was too strong to resist and Joey threw himself into the garden. He fluttered down towards the lawn but before he reached it he flapped his wings and soared up into the open sky.

Higher and higher he flew, a bright blue flash against a bright blue sky, until his wings ached like they had never ached before. Once a week he had flown round the room while his owner had cleaned his cage. Once a week he had flapped from the chair to the curtains, from the curtains to the sideboard and then back to his cage. Attacking his reflection in his mirror was all the exercise he had ever had. And now there were no bars any more. Now he was free.

He looked down at the house he had escaped from. In the back garden the woman who had kept him imprisoned all those years was running round her garden calling his name. Joey flew down into the top of a tall tree in the next garden and rested. Everywhere was so big that he couldn't take it all in. As far as he could see in any direction there was more and more to look at. It just seemed to go on for ever with no walls or doors or windows anywhere.

'I wonder where they hang their pictures,' he thought.

'Hello, Joey,' he said, 'who's a pretty boy?'

Below him in the wild garden some sparrows were hopping about in the grass picking up seeds, so Joey flew down to see them. At first they took no notice of him but after he'd asked them who was a pretty boy for the fiftieth time they could ignore him no longer.

'Well, not you,' said one of the sparrows.

'Yes,' said another, 'who ever heard of a bird that was coloured blue?'

'What?' said Joey. 'Hello, Joey. Who's a pretty boy?'

'What's the matter with him?' said the first sparrow. 'Is he a bit simple?'

'Joey's a clever boy,' said Joey.

'Maybe he fell in a tin of blue paint and swallowed some,' said a third sparrow.

'Hello, Joey,' said the poor confused budgie. 'Someone at the door, someone at the door.'

'I think we should attack him,' said one of the sparrows. 'That's what sparrows do to strange birds isn't it?'

'Only if they're smaller than us,' said the first sparrow. 'I'm not going near him, not with that beak.'

'Time for Joey's bath. Joey's a clever boy,' said Joey and jumped into Rosie the dog's water bowl. This wouldn't have been too bad except that Rosie was asleep on the grass right next to her water bowl, and Joey's vigorous splashing soon woke her up. The sparrows flew off to the bottom of the garden as Rosie stood up and shook herself.

'Hello, Joey,' said the wet budgie, hopping out of the water.

Rosie leant forward and sniffed Joey. He was the most beautiful bird she had ever seen, as blue as the sky, just like a dream.

'Woof, woof,' said Joey.

'What?' said Rosie.

'Sorry,' said Joey, 'it's a habit. I imitate everyone.'

'Gosh, that's clever,' said Rosie. 'Who were you doing then?'

'When?'

'When you said woof, woof?' said Rosie.

'You,' said Joey. 'Joey's a clever boy. Time for Joey's bath.'

'Woof, woof?' said Rosie. 'I don't say woof, woof.'

Joey explained that was how dogs sounded to humans.

'No, no,' said Rosie, 'that's wrong. That's how humans sound to dogs.'

'No, *you've* got it the wrong way round,' said Joey. 'Humans say tweet, tweet all the time.'

'Can we talk about something else?' asked Rosie.

Just then Joey's human put her head over the fence and pleaded softly and gently with him.

'*Come to mummy, there's a good boy,*' she said. '*Come to mummy.*'

'See,' said Joey. 'I told you they say tweet, tweet, tweet.'

'That one didn't,' said Rosie. 'She just said woof, woof, woof.'

As soon as Rosie spoke, Joey's human jumped up and down behind the fence and waved her hands around.

'*Help, help,*' she screamed. '*That awful dog's*

going to eat my baby.'

'Tweet, tweet,' shouted Joey and flew into the bushes.

'Woof, woof,' shouted Rosie and ran after her.

'*Oh, my precious baby,*' cried Joey's human and ran off into her house.

'Who on earth's that awful woman?' said Rosie. 'She whinges a lot doesn't she?'

'She used to keep me inside her house, locked up in a tiny cage,' said Joey.

'That's awful,' said Rosie. 'Nobody should be locked up.'

'I know,' said Joey. 'I used to sit at the bars and look out into the garden and feel so lonely.'

'Well you don't have to be lonely now,' said Rosie. 'I'll be your friend.'

'Woof, woof,' said Joey.

'Tweet, tweet,' said Rosie.

'Still, it wasn't all bad,' said Joey. 'I had a lovely mirror.'

The back door of the house opened and the two children came rushing out with Joey's owner. They ran around the lawn looking into the bushes and up through the branches. Rosie ran out into the open to distract them while Joey flew down and hid in the thick brambles by the canal.

'*Oh, oh,*' Joey's owner cried, '*your horrible little dog's eaten my beautiful baby.*'

Joey heard her and flew back across the lawn in case her new friend got into trouble. He flew up and landed on the gutter looking down at them.

'Who's a pretty boy?' he called out, just in case they hadn't seen him.

'*There he is,*' shouted the children.

'Joey's a clever boy,' said Joey.

'*Joey, come to mummy, there's a good boy,*' she said. '*Come to mummy.*'

The children tried to hide their grinning faces from the woman. She sounded so stupid and they felt quite sorry for Joey. Rosie ran round and round barking and jumping in the air. The children's mother came out but she had no more sympathy for the woman than her children. Everyone at the house called fourteen was definitely on Joey's side. They didn't like animals being locked up and they weren't going to change their minds for Joey's owner.

'*You just go home,*' said the children's mother, '*and we'll see if we can lure him into the house with a nice bit of cuttlefish.*'

'Cuttlefish, I'm sick to death of cuttlefish,' said Joey, when he saw it sitting on the kitchen window sill. 'Whoever got the idea that budgerigars like cuttlefish? What do they think we do, deep sea dive for it, swim under water with a sharp knife and kill squid?'

'Yeah,' said Rosie, 'quite right. What's a cuttlefish?'

Joey spent the rest of the afternoon flying around the garden eating things. After a lifetime of eating the same old boring bird seed every single day, it was like being in a giant supermarket. There was so much to choose from. At first he followed the other birds and ate what they were eating. While it meant eating grass seeds and peanuts in the bird feeder it was alright, everything tasted wonderful, fresh and exciting. When it meant poking about in the grass for slugs, he wasn't quite so sure. His beak was the wrong shape and all he got were mouthfuls of mud. When he finally did manage to eat a slug, he decided the mud was better. It took a lot of drinking and spitting in the pond to get rid of the awful slimy taste.

He drove all the other birds mad with his endless chattering. It wasn't just that they hadn't the faintest idea what he was talking about, it was more that he kept saying the same thing over and over again. By the end of the day every single animal in the garden knew that he was a pretty boy, he was a clever boy and that there was someone at the door.

'I don't care how dangerous his beak looks,' said one of the sparrows, 'if he tells me once more what a pretty boy he is, I'll kill him.'

'Yeah,' said another, 'he's driving me mad.'

'Maybe we should get the cuckoos to have a go at him,' said a third.

'No, they like him,' said the first sparrow. 'Every

time they go near him, he just imitates them.'

As dusk fell all the animals began to go to their beds. Rosie went indoors for her supper and then curled up on someone's lap. The sparrows that weren't sitting on eggs, perched on branches next to their nests and one by one most of the other birds settled down for the night. A family of swans out on the canal floated slowly through the water, their long necks curved gracefully round as they tucked their heads back under their wings and slept. Only the owls were different. For them it was time to wake up. Other animals were beginning their days too. The rabbits came to the mouths of their burrows and sniffed the air, while the hedgehogs scrambled out from under the shed and began to crash about through the long grass. Everyone had somewhere to go. Everyone, that is, except Joey.

Joey had never really seen the night before. Sometimes when his owner had forgotten to close the curtains he'd sat in his cage and looked out at the darkening sky, but there had always been a light on in the room. Outside the window had just been like looking at a painting. Now he was inside that painting and he didn't know what to do. It was getting cold too and that was something Joey had never felt before.

As the sun set, the shape of the trees grew sharp against the dark gold sky. The leaves and branches changed from green and brown to deep black and Joey felt his beak begin to chatter. He fluffed up his feathers and flew from branch to branch but no one wanted him. Everyone had their place and Joey's place was next door in a chromium cage.

'Go away,' said the sparrows.

'There's no room here,' said the blackbirds.

'This is private property,' said the robin.

'Ooh, breakfast,' said Dennis the Owl. 'I've never had blue breakfast before.'

The sky grew darker until the only light was the warm gold glow from the house windows. Great dark clouds rolled across the sky covering the moon and stars. Joey flew down onto the lawn and stood in the pool of light from the french windows. And as he stood there it began to rain.

'Not time for Joey's bath,' he said as the cold water soaked through to his skin.

'You look wet,' said a terrifying round prickly thing. It was Barry the hedgehog. Joey had never seen a hedgehog and thought Barry was the weirdest looking creature he'd ever seen.

'Are you a nightmare?' he said, shivering with cold and fear.

'No, of course not,' said Barry. 'I'm a hedgehog and if you stand out here in the pouring rain, you'll either die of cold or the owls will get you.'

'I've got nowhere to go,' said Joey. 'Everyone keeps chasing me away.'

'Follow me,' said Barry. 'I know someone who'll look after you.'

Barry walked across the lawn towards the bottom of the garden and Joey walked slowly after him. The hedgehog had to keep waiting for the wet budgerigar to catch up because the bird could hardly see in the darkness. When they reached the chicken hut, Barry went inside and across to Ethel's nest. The old chicken was sitting fluffed up staring into the darkness.

'I just don't seem to be able to get to sleep any more,' she said.

Barry told her what had happened and Ethel was only too happy to help.

'I've sat on all sorts of things in my time,' she said, 'but never a blue bird.'

Joey hopped up into Ethel's nesting box and the old chicken tucked him under her wing. He told her everything that had happened since his escape that morning, how wonderful it had felt to be free, but how it had all changed when night had fallen.

'What I can't understand,' said Ethel, 'is why you want to be free. I certainly don't.'

'But you are free,' said Joey. 'You can go wherever you like and you can do whatever you feel like doing.'

'But I don't,' said Ethel, 'and I don't want to. I want to belong to someone. I like knowing that there are people who will look after me.' And she told Joey about the time when the house had been deserted and how lonely she had felt.

'I mean, everyone's so nice to you, aren't they?' she said.

'Oh yes,' said Joey, 'I get food and water every day and I've got a lovely mirror with another budgie in it just like me and when I sing to him, he sings to me.'

'Well then,' said Ethel.

'Yes, but I'm not free,' said Joey.

'To do what?' said Ethel. 'Get soaked through and eaten by owls?'

'Yes,' said Joey. 'Well, er, no.'

They talked on and on until the morning and Joey knew, as he had done from the start really, that being free was as much about how you felt inside your head as it was about flying through the trees. Like the swans belonged on the river and the sparrows belonged in the trees, so Joey knew that he belonged next door in a shiny silver cage with a beautiful mirror and a lovely piece of cuttlefish. He'd been in the trees. He'd had a wonderful adventure, but now it was time to go home.

He flew out of the chicken hut up into the sky as far as he could go. The world was waking up and the air was still cold with the chill of night. Down below he could see his home and it looked safe and inviting. He wanted to say goodbye to Rosie but there was no sign of her as he flew down into the trees in the wild garden.

The window next door was open, the window he had flown out of the day before.

'Joey, come on,' said a voice inside his head. 'Come home.'

And he did.

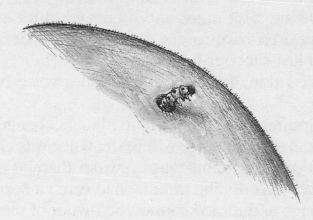

Godfrey the Maggot

Godfrey the maggot ate his way deeper into the peach. All around him everything was soft and wet and golden. Behind him a warm breeze tickled his back but as he tunnelled deeper into the fruit the air grew cool and still. He had been eating his way backwards and forwards through the peach for his whole life, all three days of it. In that time he had seen the whole world from the bright light shining through the skin to the dark mysteries of the centre with its magnificent stone. In all that time he had never seen another living soul. Every day he grew fatter and happier and the tunnels he made grew wider and wider. The whole peach was all his and he felt pretty pleased and important.

'Life is completely brilliant,' he said. 'How many animals can eat their own homes?'

He ate a bit more and then said, 'I mean, you don't even have to get out of bed for breakfast. You just eat your bed.'

'You don't half talk a lot,' said a voice behind him.

Godfrey jumped so hard that he banged his head. He tried to see where the voice was coming from but the tunnel was no wider than he was so he couldn't. By the time he had eaten a space big enough and turned round, the owner of the voice had gone. All Godfrey could see was another tunnel cutting right across his own. He looked down it but it was quite empty. He ate himself back round again and carried on the way he had been going. In front of him it grew lighter and Godfrey knew he was reaching the other side of the peach again. He started eating an extra mouthful to the right each time and gradually began to turn back towards the middle.

'Round we go,' he said. 'Round we go.'

'Don't you ever stop talking?' asked the voice behind him again.

Once again Godfrey ate a space to turn round in, and once again there was no one there, just the tunnel crossing his own. He turned back and carried on.

'I'll keep really quiet,' he said to himself. 'Really, really quiet and then I'll catch him.'

As he got near the centre of the world he crossed another tunnel, but instead of going by, he went down it.

'If I go really fast,' he thought, 'I'll catch up with whoever it is.'

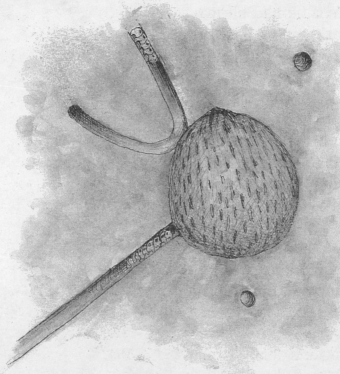

He wriggled down the tunnel as fast as he could. It was a strange feeling, not eating, and Godfrey began to feel uncomfortable. The tunnel stretched ahead of him in a long curve that never seemed to end. He shut his eyes and wriggled faster and faster until he came to a sudden end and smashed his head against the peach stone.

Maggots don't have hard things in their
heads like skulls, so when they bang
their heads their brains wobble
around like frightened jellies.
Godfrey would have seen
stars if he had known
what they were but as
all he had ever seen
was fruit, that was
what he saw. His
head spun and he
saw fruit.

'You're stupid as
well as noisy,'
laughed the
voice behind
him. Godfrey
spun round and
saw the back end
of another
maggot wriggling
off down the tunnel.

This went on for several
days and as it did so
Godfrey felt the peach begin
to get softer. The juice was
becoming a problem too. At first he
could just drink it but now the tunnels were

running wet and sticky. With every bite the whole place got wetter and wetter. In some places the tunnels were completely flooded and Godfrey had to eat through soft brown patches that tasted awful and collapsed around him.

'It's the end of the world,' he said.

'It's time to pupate,' said the voice, but this time it was right in front of him. There looking straight at him was himself, or what he imagined himself to look like.

'Who are you?' he asked.

'Godfrey,' said the other maggot.

'But *I'm* Godfrey,' said Godfrey.

'We all are,' said twenty other maggots that had appeared from various tunnels.

'Yes, and we'd better get out of here, quickly,' said the first stranger, 'before this whole thing comes crashing down around us.'

The twenty-two fat maggots bit their way through the peach skin and crawled out bleary-eyed into the sunshine. Above their heads the golden light danced and sparkled through the nettle leaves. Below them the grass shone like a soft quilt. It was the most beautiful sight they had ever seen.

'Is this heaven?' said the first Godfrey.

'I think it must be,' said one of the others.

They all thought it was heaven, and so did the happy blue budgerigar as he ate twenty-two fat juicy maggots for breakfast.

Bert the Crow

Bert the crow sat in the top of the tallest tree of the garden and looked down through the branches. It was a beautiful spring day. The buds were starting to open but the leaves were still small enough to give a clear view down into the garden. On the lawn, the soft round shape of Ethel the chicken waddled slowly about pecking between the blades of grass. Even so far above ground Bert could see the slugs and worms as they sparkled in the sunlight. He had been out on the motorway all morning and although the slugs looked particularly tasty in the midday sun, Bert couldn't have eaten another mouthful.

'What was that you were eating this morning, our Bert?' said his mother.

'I haven't the faintest idea, mother,' said Bert. 'It was black. I know that.'

'Furs or feathers?' asked his mother.

'Fur, I think,' said Bert. 'I was too busy dodging the cars to pay much attention.'

'True enough, lad,' said Bert's dad. 'The roads were right busy this morning.'

'I'll tell you one thing though,' said Bert. 'Whatever it was I was eating, it was right flat.'

'Aye, lad,' said his father. 'It were dead flat.' And they all laughed.

'The flatter the better, I reckon,' said Bert. 'There's nothing like a few heavy lorries rolling over it to make your dinner nice and tender.'

'True enough, lad,' said Bert's dad. 'The heavier the better.'

'Tell us about the two-metre hedgehog, our Dad,' said Bert's mum. 'You know the one the railway engine ran over.'

'Nay, lass, it was a huge eighty-four wheeler lorry with a train on the back, what did it,' said Bert's dad. 'That poor hedgehog was over two metres long and it was so flat you could see daylight through it.'

'Was it flatter than that squirrel we had on Sunday?' asked Bert.

'Oh aye, lad,' said Bert's dad. 'That squirrel was like Mount Everest compared to the two-metre hedgehog. Why it was so thin it rustled in the breeze.'

'Eeee,' said Bert's mum.

'Aye,' said Bert's dad.

'What did it look like, dad?' said Bert. 'Could you read a book through it?'

'Well, I never actually saw it myself, lad,' said Bert's dad, 'but I'm sure you could.'

Bert's dad didn't actually know what a book was but he wasn't going to let Bert know that.

The three crows sat in the afternoon sunshine and day-dreamed. Bert's mum dreamt about the old days when the factories across the canal had been a hive of activity. Big lorries with fat tyres had been in and out all day long and food had been plentiful, and flat. Bert dreamed of finding the flattest widest meal there had ever been, a meal that was spread so thin you could hardly see it, a meal that would make the two-metre hedgehog look like a door mat. And Bert's dad just sat with his eyes closed and hoped no one would find out that the two-metre hedgehog was just a story his father had told him when he was a little fledgling. It had been an old story then. His father had heard it from his grandfather and one day Bert's dad supposed he would have to tell Bert that it was just a story, but not yet.

'Those were the days,' said Bert's mum.
'Aye, lass,' said Bert's dad. 'The flat old days.'

The days were really beginning to feel warm again now. There had been time in the middle of winter when it seemed as if it would be cold forever, but now you could tell that summer was on its way. The two older crows turned their faces up to the warmth of the sunshine and soon fell fast asleep.

Bert was bored. He didn't want to sit around all afternoon. He kept thinking about the two-metre hedgehog. He tried to imagine how it must have tasted. To us the thought of a poor hedgehog rolled out like a tablecloth is rather horrible, but to Bert it seemed as delicious as a strawberry tart covered in thick cream and custard and chocolate flakes and fudge sauce and sugar.

He flew up above the house and out across the canal to the factories on the far side. Most of them were deserted now, with broken windows and rusting steel roofs. There were weeds growing up through the split concrete where cars and lorries had once parked. Inside the old buildings the air was still and silent. The machines and desks had been taken away years before and all that was left now were rusty marks on dusty floors and faded yellow notices pinned to peeling doors. Mice and spiders were the kings and queens in this forgotten landscape. A few birds nested in broken walls. Half-starved, half-wild cats roamed the corridors hunting half-starved rats, and the occasional fox passed through but there was nothing there for crows.

There were still a few factories working. They looked almost as tired as the ones that were closed down and there were no big lorries anywhere to squash something juicy with. There were a few cars and a couple of fork lift trucks but that was about it. There was nothing moving that would squash anything really flat.

Bert flew on beyond
the industrial estate,
past the three-
hundred-feet-tall
chimney. There
were a lot of big
machines parked on
some empty land
but none of them
were moving and
beyond that there
were just more
houses. As it started
to get dark he
turned for home.
His parents were
still sitting on the
gutter at the back of
the house, still
muttering away in
their daydreams.
Bert flew into the
tall tree where they
all roosted and fell
asleep.

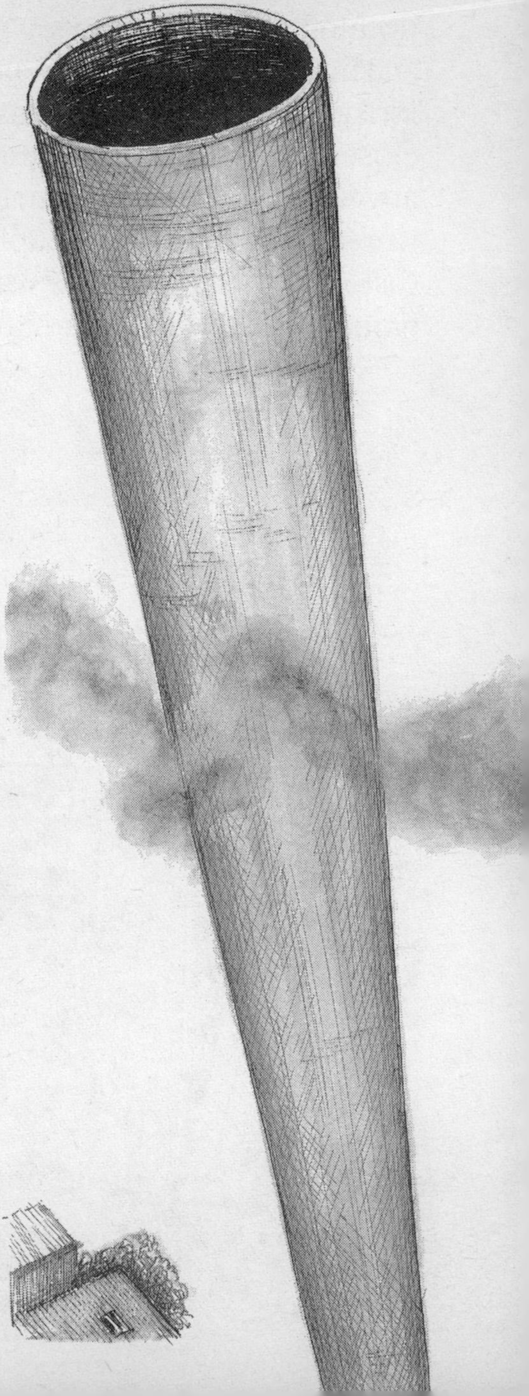

The next morning a passing crow told them about the new roadworks that had started by the old chimney.

'And we all know what that means, don't we?' said the visitor.

'Aye, lad,' said Bert's dad, 'lots of big machines, lots of big fat heavy tyres to squash things.'

'Aye, breakfast,' said Bert's mum.

For the next few months there was plenty to eat and everyone grew fat and happy. Bert's mum hatched out four new eggs and was busy feeding them all day. Bert spent every day, until it was almost too dark to see, hanging round the roadworks with a gang of other crows. Sometimes there was so much great flat stuff to eat it was too dark to get home by the time they'd finished and they'd all spend the night inside the three-hundred foot chimney.

But all the time Bert couldn't get the thought of the two-metre hedgehog out of his mind. He told his mates about the two-metre hedgehog but they all seemed to know about it already.

'It's just a story,' said Eddie. Eddie was a flash bird from the roughest part of town and all the others were a bit afraid of him. If you had any sense you didn't argue with Eddie.

'Are you sure?' said Bert. 'My dad reckons it's true.'

'Yeah, well so does my dad,' said Eddie, 'but he's never seen it.'

'No, neither has mine,' said Bert.

'I reckon it's all made up,' said Eddie.

'You're probably right,' said Bert.

Bert couldn't really believe that Eddie was right. To do that would mean he'd have to say his dad had lied to him and he couldn't imagine him ever doing that.

'Eddie's dad probably just heard about it from someone who had told someone else about someone who had heard it from his cousin's uncle's friend,' he thought. 'That's why Eddie doesn't believe it.'

The roadworks were coming to an end but that was the best time. That was the time they brought in the steam-rollers and then things got *really* flat. Not many things got squashed but when they did they were the sweetest things any of them had ever tasted. Bert's flattest meal was pink, or rather it had started off pink but by the time Bert got it it was a dirty grey colour.

The steam-roller driver had spat it out onto the fresh black tarmac as he had climbed up into the cab and then he'd driven over it. Bert had seen it but when the machine had passed it had vanished. At first he thought someone else had got it, but the others had gone to the station for the day to scavenge round the trains. He looked all over the road but the pink stuff had gone. He looked after the roller and there it was, stuck to the great steel front wheel, and every time the machine rolled forward the pink stuff got flatter and flatter.

Bert hopped after the steam-roller all morning, watching the amazing meal get wider and thinner with every turn. When the machine stopped for lunch it had got so thin and picked up so much dirt that it was almost invisible.

'Oh wow,' said Bert. 'It must be a million times thinner than the two-metre hedgehog.'

And it was, but when he pecked and peeled it off the wheel it was awful. It collapsed into a disgusting wriggling mess that stuck to his feathers and glued his beak together.

'Ee look, our dad,' said Bert's mum, 'our Bert's got his first chewing gum.'

'Aye, lass, that takes me back,' said Bert's dad.

'Flat enough for you, is it?' said Bert's mum and the two crows fell out of the tree from laughing.

'Nnnnn . . . nnnn thh,' said Bert, scraping his beak along the branch over and over again.

It was two days before he finally got rid of the last of it and by then he was starving. He flew back to the roadworks but everything was gone. There was one small van and a few men poking around near the three-hundred-foot chimney but all the big machines were gone.

'I'm so hungry,' Bert said to himself, 'that I could eat something fat.'

He sat on top of the chimney and peered down and there far below at the foot of the tower was a tiny white speck. Bert slid off the ledge and floated down towards it. There, lying in the grass was a big thick ham sandwich. As he got near the ground a rat crawled out from a gap in the bricks and grabbed it. It chewed and tore at it and tried to pull it into the gap, but before it could and before Bert could reach it, the whole world exploded with the greatest explosion anyone had ever heard.

Bert was thrown outwards as the whole tower came crashing down on itself. In a great cloud of bricks and dust he was hurled across the wasteland and fell in a filthy heap on the ground. Miraculously not a single piece of brick had touched him and apart from being grey instead of black and having a dreadful headache, he was completely unharmed.

The tower was not unharmed. When the dust had cleared Bert could see the magnificent building was now nothing more than a sad pile of broken bricks. He remembered all the days he had sat on the top of the tower with his family and his mates looking out across the whole town. On clear summer days you could see right into the countryside, see the soft green hills rolling away into a distant blue haze and in the other direction the hills turned to valleys that slipped softly down to the sea. It was all so sad.

For three weeks men with lorries cleared the broken tower away. Bert sat on a nearby factory every day and watched them. He felt that until every single brick had gone he ought to watch over the last days of the three-hundred foot chimney. He knew that it was what he had to do.

When the last lorry left, Bert flew up into the sky above the tower's ghost and when he reached the place where the top had been he looked down at the ground. And there below him was the sandwich and still holding on to it was the rat. Only now the sandwich was no longer a white speck, it was as wide as a double bed, and the rat was as long as a carpet and compared to them the two-metre hedgehog, true or not, seemed as thick as Eddie.

Bert drifted slowly down on the warm air taking in the wonderful sight of the flattest meal there had ever been in the whole history of any universe. For nearly an hour he floated round and round until at last he landed in the middle of the most perfect meal he had ever seen, a meal so thin that to anyone else it would have been invisible. He flew around its edge in both directions. He flew back up into the sky for one last look and then when the afternoon sun had warmed it all to perfection he came down to eat.

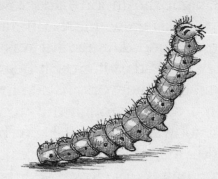

Venus the Caterpillar

Venus the caterpillar crawled out from under the tomato plant leaf in the greenhouse and looked up at the stars. Low in the evening sky was a thin silver crescent, too small to cast a shadow but as delicate as a piece of fine jewellery. Venus had never seen the moon before and she couldn't take her eyes off it.

'It's the most beautiful thing I've ever seen,' she said, but no one else seemed very interested.

'Oh yes,' sneered Gilbert the cockroach, 'and what other beautiful things have you seen?'

'Leaves,' said Venus, 'and stalks and other things.'

'Like what?'

'A flowerpot,' said Venus, 'I've seen a flower-pot.'

'You're pathetic,' said Gilbert and scuttled off to eat some compost.

The next night the moon had grown and the night after that it grew more. In fact, it kept growing for days and days until it was as big and round as the sun. And as it grew it began to cast a cool blue light over the world. When it was full, its beams poured down through the trees and sent long dark shadows across the lawn, bathing the whole world in peaceful silence. Everything looked frozen in its cool glow. Even the tomatoes above Venus's head shone blue like little moons themselves. She looked up through the leaves and knew that no matter what she did she had to go to the moon. She didn't know that one day she would have wings and be able to fly, nor did she know that when she could fly she would then find out just how incredibly far away the moon was. She just knew she had to get there.

'If I went outside,' she said, 'and climbed to the top of the tallest tree, right to the very end of the highest leaf, do you think I could reach it?'

'Oh yeah,' scoffed Gilbert, 'if you waited like a million years for the tree to grow until it was a thousand million miles tall.'

'Really? That's great,' said Venus. 'How long's a million years?'

'Give me strength,' cried Gilbert, banging his head against a sleeping slug and getting his feelers all sticky.

'Well, how long *is* a million years?' said Venus. 'Is it longer than tomorrow and today all put together?'

Gilbert muttered something under his breath about wishing he was carnivorous and vanished. Venus couldn't see what all the fuss was about. It all seemed quite simple. By the time she got out of the greenhouse, the tree would have already grown quite a lot and by the time she climbed to the end of the very highest leaf, it probably would be a million years old.

'I suppose,' she said to anyone who would listen, 'there's always the possibility that the tree will grow faster than I can climb it and I suppose it could take so long to get there that by the time I do, the tree could be taller than the moon and I'd have to come down a bit.'

Gilbert was swearing underneath the table but Venus couldn't make out what he was saying. It didn't matter anyway. She didn't know that cockroaches were nasty sarcastic creatures. She just thought Gilbert was being helpful.

Venus said goodbye to all her brothers and sisters and set off straight away. She crawled down the tomato plant stalk, down the outside of the flowerpot and wriggled to the edge of the table. She stopped and looked back at her home, wondering if she'd ever see it or her family again. As she turned to go on, she glanced up at the beautiful moon and almost fainted.

It was shrinking. All down one side it had
vanished. Venus couldn't believe it. Her great big
beautiful moon was dying and it was dying so fast
that it would be gone before she could get there.

'If only I could reach it in time,' she said, 'I might be able to make it well again.'

'You are the most stupid caterpillar I've ever met,' said Gilbert. 'No, wait a minute. That's not true. Every caterpillar I've ever met, and I've met hundreds, has been just as stupid as you are.'

'But the moon is dying,' said Venus.

'No it isn't,' said Gilbert. 'It does that every month. It gets bigger and then it gets smaller and then it gets bigger again.'

'Are you sure?' said Venus.

'Are caterpillars horrid little creatures that look like the outsides of their bodies are missing? Of course I'm sure,' said Gilbert.

'So if I climb the tree it will come back again and I'll be able to go there?' said Venus.

'Yeah, yeah, sure,' said Gilbert and scuttled off again.

'Why do I keep doing this?' he said as he hurried across the greenhouse floor. 'Why do I keep having conversations with these idiots? Why don't I stay at home and do something I'd enjoy more, like hitting my head against the wall?'

Venus slipped over the edge and began to crawl towards the floor, but when she reached the underneath of the table a strange feeling began to come over her. It was a feeling that she had never felt before, a sort of weird sense that something incredible was going to happen.

'Isn't it lovely under here?' she thought even though she couldn't see her beloved moon. 'I think I'd like to have a little sleep right where I am.'

Part of her thought she should go on. After all, it was quite a long way to the moon so she shouldn't waste any time. But a stronger feeling seemed to be overtaking her and that told her it was time for bed. The more she tried to sort out her thoughts, the more tired she became until she just *had* to go to sleep. She spun a tiny silk thread, fixed it to the underneath of the table and soon fell fast asleep. And as she slept, strange and incredible things happened to her.

Venus the moth yawned and stretched. Inside her head she was still Venus the caterpillar but on the outside she was now Venus the moth. Of course, she didn't know this yet. She still thought she was a caterpillar and that she had just nodded off to sleep for a bit. It had been dark when she had gone to sleep and it was still dark now, so she thought it was the same day. In fact, a whole winter had passed. She had gone to sleep in the autumn and now it was early spring.

'Better get on, I suppose,' she thought to herself and stretched to her full length. 'Got to get to the moon.'

Suddenly there was a loud splitting noise and Venus felt a blast of cool air. She felt blood moving through places she didn't remember having. There were hairs all over her body where she had been smooth and shiny.

'I'm sure they weren't there when I went to sleep,' she said, peering back at a pair of pale wings. 'I'd have noticed them.'

She waved the new wings and found she was hovering in mid air.

'Oh wow,' she thought, 'this is brilliant.'

And she realised that she wouldn't have to climb all the way up the tree to reach the moon. She could just fly there. It was incredible.

'I won't have to wait a million years any more,' she said. 'I'll just be able to fly there in half an hour.'

She looked up into the sky and there was the beautiful moon. Only it looked different from before. When she had been a caterpillar, it had seemed enormous and had looked as if it was an extremely long way away. Now she was a moth it looked quite small and very close.

'Funny that,' she thought and flew up to the top of the greenhouse roof for a better look. And it *was* very close, and instead of being cool and blue it was now warm and pale gold and it had a name and its name was 40Watts.

'It's even more beautiful close up,' said Venus.

Every night she flew to the moon. Every night she flew round and round it and the amazing thing was that it never got smaller again. Venus knew then that Gilbert the cockroach had been wrong. All that stuff about the moon getting bigger and smaller had just been rubbish. The moon had been dying and she knew that by flying up to it she had made it well again. After all, if that wasn't the case then why would she have woken up with a pair of wings?

Moonlight

The sky has no clouds on this dark night
And people sleep deep in their beds.
Children are dreaming
And the dogs at their feet
Run through old days in their heads.

The sky has no clouds but millions of stars,
Other suns with worlds of their own.
Round each one a moon
Might look down through its trees.
So why do we feel so alone?

The sky has no clouds on this dark night
And moonlight runs over the town.
Its shadows are dark
Giving places to hide
As the owl flies across looking down.

The sky has no clouds but millions of stars,
And a dog looks up at the moon
And it howls at the light
Like its ancestors did
For the spinechilling dawn coming soon.

Ethel's Dreamtime

The long hot summer began to slip away. At first it was barely noticeable, no more than a slight fading of the trees and a softness in the grass as if nature was getting tired and wanted a rest. Plants that had stood tall and proud began to hang their heads and give up their seeds to the wind. Ethel the chicken felt tired too. Autumn was creeping into her bones and, like the plants, she felt weary. Like them she had grown old and slow. She had seen it all before many times and now she just wanted to sleep.

'You're the oldest animal in the garden,' said Arthur the rabbit. He had lived for twelve years and all his life Ethel had been there. Even back in his earliest memory she had been old.

'In fact,' he said, 'you are probably the oldest chicken in the world.'

Ethel didn't really understand what Arthur was talking about. She was a chicken and being old didn't mean anything to her. Yesterday was just like last week only not so fuzzy round the edges. A few things remained in her memory. There was Eric the cockerel who had been so proud and strong and there was a picture in her mind from long ago of an old lady stroking her head. And she could remember a time when the grass had grown tall and the garden had become a jungle. They had been exciting days. All the other animals had thrived in those years and many new creatures had come to live in the garden, but Ethel had felt lonely. The house had been empty apart from rats and spiders. The windows had been dark every night and the doors had stayed locked and closed.

'It all feels so lonely without anyone living here,' she had said.

'It's peaceful,' said the other animals, 'and safe.'

'I miss them,' said the old chicken.

'You just miss the food,' said the others.

'No,' Ethel had said. 'It's not the food. It's the talking. I miss the warm voices and the feeling of belonging to someone.'

'Animals shouldn't belong to anyone,' said the others. 'We're wild animals, we should be free.'

'I don't want to be wild or free,' Ethel had said. 'I want to belong to someone.'

Nothing the other animals said had made any difference. She'd heard them tell her about all the terrible things that people did to animals, but she had never seen any of it so it didn't really mean anything. The only humans she had ever known had been kind and she missed them.

'It's because I'm domesticated,' she used to say sadly, without really knowing what it meant.

Then everything had changed. A family had come to live in the house and the loneliness had ended. The man had given her a smart new box to live in and the children had come to see her every day. Later on they gave her eggs to hatch and she had children again, four beautiful hens called Doris and a magnificent cockerel called Doris-Boris. They had their grown-up feathers now and scratched and fussed around the garden all day. They had seen their own seasons and didn't need her any more.

The children in the house were growing up too.

Every day they brought her food and every day they tickled her behind the head. She sat in the thick warm straw at the dark end of the chicken hut and waited for them to come. Sometimes when the day was warm and the air buzzed with the hum of summer, one of the children would carry her up to the house and she would potter about in the flower beds while they sat on the steps reading books. But now winter was coming and the children stayed indoors.

'I feel so tired,' said the old chicken. 'Even when I wake up, I feel tired.'

'It's getting old does that,' said Arthur the rabbit. 'I feel the same. You need to sleep more.'

'That's all I ever do anyway,' said Ethel, 'sleep.'

But it wasn't true. She sat still a lot but she found herself sleeping less and less. As the sun went down her children came back into the hut to roost. One by one they hopped up onto the perch and huddled together clucking and muttering to themselves until they fell asleep. It was a gentle friendly noise and the air smelled warm and comfortable, but in her box at the other end of the hut Ethel sat staring through the window at the night sky. During the night the mice and rats would shuffle through the straw on the floor looking for scraps of food. Sometimes they would stop and talk to Ethel but most nights they were too busy and just ignored her. On cloudless nights an owl would fly past, its shape outlined against the moon. Ethel saw the face on the moon and she watched the stars move silently over the world as they had done for millions and millions of years. And if there were no stars she stared into the darkness until morning.

117

It had become the same every night. Sleep had left her and it had left her tired. Sometimes in the warm afternoon sunshine she would nod off for a while but the slightest thing would wake her and that would be the end of it. Now it was winter and there was no sunshine warm enough for dreams.

'I just don't seem to be able to get warm any more,' she said.

'That's old age too,' said Arthur. 'Your heart gets slow. Your blood gets thin and stands still.'

'I don't think I want any of that,' said Ethel.

'Any of what?' asked Arthur.

'Old age.'

'Well, it isn't something you can decide about,' said Arthur. 'It just happens.'

'What, even if you don't want it to?' said Ethel.

'Yes, of course,' said Arthur.

'Who told you that?' asked Ethel.

'My father,' said Arthur.

'Is that what happened to him?' said Ethel. 'Did he get old age?'

'Yes.'

'And is it like that for everyone?'

'I think so,' said Arthur.

'You mean, I'm going to be tired and cold forever?' said Ethel.

'I don't know,' said Arthur irritably. He was tired too and he didn't feel like talking about it.

Ethel sat silently in the door to the hut. She wanted to ask Arthur about his father. If he still had old age and if he found it difficult to sleep, but Arthur limped off into the bushes. Perhaps she should go and talk to Arthur's father. Perhaps he could tell her what was going to happen.

She sat there staring into space and her thoughts all faded away. Daydreaming, that's what her mother had called it.

'Stop daydreaming,' she'd said, when Ethel had been young and feeling all lazy in the sunshine.

'Why?' Ethel had asked. Her mother had never had a really good answer for that, but it had left Ethel with a feeling that sitting around doing nothing was wrong and all her life she had felt a bit guilty about doing it. Now she didn't care. Now, as she let her thoughts drift away, they really did drift away and her head became completely empty and her eyes grew lazy until everything was a blur. The sweet emptiness made up for the lack of sleep. She felt as if she could sit there for ever.

'Come on, out of the way,' shouted a voice in her ear. 'Move over, some of us have got work to do.'

It was one of her daughters, pushing past her. Ethel fell over and the younger hen ran into the hut and laid an egg.

'There's no need to rush,' said Ethel, struggling to her feet and fluffing out her feathers. 'There's more to life than laying eggs.'

'No there isn't,' said her daughter.

'Of course there is,' said Ethel. 'What about sunsets and the smell of rain on the grass? What about daydreaming?'

'Daydreaming, daydreaming?' said her daughter. 'What a waste of time.'

'What about flowers and talking to your friends? What about bacon rind?' said Ethel.

'You're going soft in the head,' said the young hen. 'You're just saying that because you *can't* lay eggs anymore.'

'No I'm not,' said Ethel, but she wasn't really sure.

'You're just saying that because you're old and useless,' said the young hen as she crashed off into the bushes.

Ethel stood staring at the floor. Maybe her daughter was right, maybe that was what life was all about, just laying eggs. The old hen climbed down from the shed and shuffled through the long grass to the pond. That was where she always went when she was feeling low.

She ignored the rabbits under the tall trees. Other animals called out good mornings as she went by but she didn't notice any of them. She dragged her feet in the earth, looked out across the canal and sighed deeply. When she reached the pond she walked in up to her knees and stood ankle deep in the mud. She stood there for hours staring at her own reflection in the water.

'Do you think I'm old and useless?' she asked the reflection, but it said nothing.

The little creatures wriggled between her toes, as they always did, and, as always when she was miserable, she didn't notice them. Old thoughts came into her head and she remembered the feeling she had had many years ago. It was loneliness.

It was different this time. The loneliness she had felt before had been because there had been no one to love her. Now she had that. The children came every day. Whenever she was in the garden, they came and found her and carried her back to the hut and fed her. The loneliness she felt now was deep inside, a sadness for the years gone by, a dull pain for all the things she would never see again.

One of the toads came and stood beside her. He sat down in the water and looked up at Ethel.

'Beautiful, isn't it?' he said.

'What?' asked Ethel.

'All this,' said the toad.

'All what?' asked Ethel.

'This,' said the toad. 'The water, the mud, all this.'

'It's horrible,' said Ethel. 'I only come here when I'm depressed.'

'Ooh, someone got out of their nest the wrong side this morning, didn't they?' said the toad.

'Don't be stupid, warty,' said Ethel. 'There's only one way *to* get out of my nest.'

'What do you know? You're just a useless old chicken,' said the toad and disappeared into the water.

Ethel felt worse than ever. She couldn't even be miserable in peace. She went and sat on the compost heap, but it was no better. As soon as she sank into the warm slimy cabbage leaves on the top, three slugs wriggled out and started telling jokes about chickens crossing roads. Ethel ate them but it didn't make her feel any better.

She walked round the edge of the lawn until she reached the back of the house. It was deserted. The french windows were open and there was music coming from inside the room but there was no sign of anyone. Even Rosie the dog was nowhere to be seen.

Ethel clambered up the steps and looked in the doorway. It had been years since she'd been inside the house. She had forgotten all about it and now standing there, it came flooding back. She had been young then, sometimes even laying more than one egg a day, and the old lady had been living there. The room had been darker too and had smelt as old as the lady. Now it was bright and clean. In her youth Ethel had been inside sometimes. The old lady had given her cake crumbs and then carried her out into the garden again.

The old chicken walked into the room and stood in the middle of the carpet. It was soft and gentle like the grass in dreams. There was a fire dancing and sparkling in the grate and the air was warm and peaceful. Ethel stood there and felt the sleep she had wanted for so long begin to creep over her. She looked round for somewhere to settle down but there were no nests anywhere.

She walked into the hall where the air was even warmer. Something from above seemed to reach out for her. It led her towards the stairs and one by one it led her slowly up the stairs. Her legs ached and each stair seemed taller than the last but finally she reached the top and stood in a long field of green carpet. Across the hall was a half-open door. It was dark and as inviting as a summer night, and whatever it was that had called her upstairs seemed to be there inside this cupboard. She looked round the edge of the door and there in the twilight was a nest of delicate blue blankets. Ethel settled down into it and closed her eyes. Pictures of home drifted through her head, golden days when Eric the cockerel had stood beside her, summer days that had seemed to last for ever. And there he stood, as tall and proud as her memory, silhouetted against the darkness.

'Eric, is that you?' she said.

Invisible arms reached out and stroked her feathers. She felt herself as light as clouds and Ethel the chicken knew at last that it was time to sleep.

127

The Twelve Thousand Franks

Under the lawn, where the cut grass gave way to the jungle of weeds and bushes, was an ants' nest. It had been there for as long as anyone could remember. It burrowed out in all directions into the centre of the lawn itself and back into the dark tangle of fallen branches and dead leaves. Its tunnels were a never-ending bustle of activity. Twenty-four hours a day the ants were busy. Most other animals had time when they slept, but not the ants.

The mornings were worst. Living with thousands of other ants in such a small space was always noisy but at the start of the day the racket was deafening as the tunnels shook to the endless pounding of one hundred and forty-four thousand feet rushing off to work. Frank1942 didn't know the exact number but one hundred and forty-four thousand seemed like a fair guess. Of course Frank786 had lost one of his legs in a jam sandwich and there were several Sandras with two extra feet, but life was too short to be that fussy. If there were a thousand more or twenty-three less it would hardly make any difference. The noise was deafening and Frank1942 had a splitting headache.

'You're pathetic,' said anyone who would listen to him. 'Ants don't get headaches.'

'Well, I've got one,' said Frank1942.

'It's impossible,' said Sandra12996. 'You're just pretending to get off work.'

'Maybe I'm different,' said Frank1942. 'Maybe I've evolved into a new super ant.'

'What,' said Sandra12996, 'a wonderful new species that can get headaches?'

'Well, it could happen,' said Frank1942.

'A new race of ants, exactly the same as ordinary ants but with headaches,' laughed the others. 'That's brilliant.'

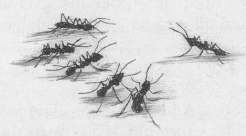

Frank1942 crept away down the tunnels to another part of the nest where he had never been before. No one understood him. He was different from all the others. He knew it, but no one else did. He knew there was more to life than rushing off to work all day following everyone else. He knew there were things like poetry and thinking. Frank1942 had never told anyone about his poetry. They wouldn't understand, they'd just laugh at him. He tried to remember his best poems. They always cheered him up.

I wandered lonely as an ant
That floats on high over tall ant hill
When all at once I saw my mum
Squashed inside an old phone bill.

He sang and

Jack and Jill went up the ant hill
To fetch a big fat larva
Jack fell down and broke his seventh knee
And Jill creased up with laughter.

And

Three blind ants, three blind ants
See how they run, See how they run
Smack into the wall.

He was still working on the last one.

'There must be more to life than this,' he said, but no one was listening.

Hundreds of ants rushed past him as he wriggled his way through the crowd in the opposite direction. His head hurt so much that he couldn't see properly. The faces of his thousands of brothers and sisters shoving past him became a blur until they all looked the same. He wanted to sit down and have a rest but there was nowhere to stop. The tunnels were filled with a wall to wall mass of busy insects.

At last, at five past nine, the rush began to ease off. Frank1942 staggered on until he could walk no further. The tunnels were almost deserted now, just a few stragglers running along to catch up with the rest.

'Hurry up, hurry up, we're late,' they called as they ran by.

Frank1942 found a crack in the tunnel wall and crept into it. He found himself in a cool dark cave full of roots, and although his head was still

hurting he soon fell asleep. In his dreams all his aches and pains faded away. The air fell silent and the tunnels were deserted. In his dreams he was the last ant on earth.

He had never been outside, up above the tunnels in the big world. He was only a second-class worker and wasn't allowed out. But he had heard about it. He'd eavesdropped on the soldier ants talking about the sunshine and the trees and giant birds that could swallow you up in one mouthful.

In his dreams he was out there right in the middle of a large red flower. He was standing ankle deep in a pool of sweet nectar. The sun shone down warm on his back and a gentle breeze drifted over the edge of the petals, tickling the hairs on his neck. It was paradise. No birds hovered in the air looking for an ant to eat. Birds, like everything else apart from Frank1942, no

longer existed. For the first time in his life he was completely alone and it was wonderful. Well, he wasn't exactly alone. On another flower was a beautiful lady ant. Frank1942 slipped over the edge petal and crawled down the stalk towards the lady ant's flower. As he started to climb again, his dream exploded and he woke up to find the

world crashing down around him.

Sandra3687 looked out across the world. From the blade of grass she was hanging onto, a sea of green spread out in all directions right off into a distant haze. It was the first time she had ever been on the surface. Until that morning she had lived in the soft brown tunnels that spread out under the lawn. Each day she had rushed off to work with everyone else and hadn't even known that there was a world above. But then, with no warning, everything had changed. Suddenly the world had come crashing down and a few seconds later she had seen the sky.

She knew what had happened. Old ants had told of the day when The Gardener would come, when their world would come to a sudden and violent end. Sandra3687 had never believed it. She had thought they were just stories to make them work harder, but now it had happened. The Gardener *had* come and destroyed their home.

All around her in the relics of her home were the remains of her brothers and sisters. She alone had survived the disaster. She wondered about other parts of the nest, if it had been the same there, if she was now the only ant left alive in the whole world.

'Hello,' she shouted, but no one answered. She climbed down from the grass and set off in no particular direction. She thought it best to get as far away from the broken nest as possible in case whatever had happened, happened again. There were some big red flowers in the distance and she set off through the grass towards them.

It was all new and frightening. The sky was filled with large dark shapes that covered the sun with giant shadows as they passed. Sandra3687 kept stopping and looking nervously over her shoulder. It wasn't being out in the world that was so scary, it was the fact that she was all alone. To make herself feel braver, she tried to think of all her brothers and sisters and pretend that they were just out of sight behind her. When she had felt afraid in the past she had always felt better when she recited her best poems. They always cheered her up.

Humpty Ant sat on the wall
Humpty Ant had a great fall
All the King's horses
And all the King's men
Trod on him

she sang and

Sweet Claire was a lovely young ant
Who was clever and quite elegant.
She said it's quite clear
I can see to next year
Because I am a Clairvoyant.

And

Baa, baa, black ant
Have you any wool?
Yes sir, yes sir,
No, hang on a minute.
No, of course I haven't
I'm an ant, stupid.

She was still working on that one.
'Hello, is there anyone there?' she called but
there was no reply.

Frank1942 knew what had happened. The Gardener had come to punish them all for not working hard enough. Frank1942 shook the dust off his back and looked around. It was incredible, it was just like his dream. He had landed in the middle of a large red flower and the dust he had been covered in wasn't the remains of his home at all. It was sweet golden pollen. Like the dream, the sun was shining and a gentle breeze was blowing through the leaves. He looked around but unlike the dream there was no beautiful lady ant on another flower. He was all alone.

'Perhaps she's been held up,' he thought. 'If I wait, she'll probably be along in a minute.'

'Hello, is there anyone there?' he called but there was no reply. He lay down in the warm sunshine and was soon fast asleep.

'Hello, is there anyone there?' Sandra3687 shouted, but there wasn't. She picked her way through the tall grass all afternoon until at last she reached the clump of red flowers. She climbed up onto one of the petals and looked round, but she was all alone. She called again but there was no reply.

Hidden in the middle of his flower and fast asleep, Frank1942 heard nothing. He slept so deeply that even the thunderstorm that came in the evening didn't wake him. By then Sandra3687 had gone. She had run up a wooden plank, across an old chicken's foot and out of the garden to the canal bank. There she had found another ants' nest, changed her name to Muriel47889 and settled down to live happily ever after.

And as for Frank1942, the next morning a child picked the flower he was sleeping on and put it in a vase on the kitchen window sill. For the rest of his life Frank1942 lived in the back of a drawer in a home of dishcloths and sponges that tickled his feet. For breakfast he ate cake crumbs with marmalade and for dinner he ate cake crumbs with strawberry jam. Every evening he looked out through the window at the wild garden. Across the lawn the ants had built a new nest but it was too far away for Frank1942 to see it. Besides, he had no time to worry about what was going on outside. He had his poetry to work on and was far too busy trying to find new words that rhymed with ant.

Full Circle

In gardens all over the town, people raked up gold and brown leaves into great piles and the evening air was filled with the soft sweet smoke of autumn bonfires. Birds tired from a summer raising children huddled in the branches and waited for winter.

And as it had done since the beginning of time, winter followed autumn and the days grew short and cold. The sun stayed low in the sky, its light weak and tired, and it gave out so little heat that the heavy frost lay undisturbed from dawn to dusk. Every twig, every blade of grass, was held in suspended animation and an intense cold crept into every corner.

As the winter sunk deeper into the earth so the animals that lived in its heart dug down below it. Some animals had flown away to warmer lands while those that were left did the best they could to survive. Some curled up in their beds and slept. Others sat it out and waited for spring.

Soon winter passed and the air was crowded with anticipation. Sleepers awoke, plants began to move and in the late spring it began to rain, not the destroying rain of winter but a hesitant rain that carried the promise of summer. A delicate uncertain rain fell in tiny drops, so small that you could barely see them. They hovered in the air like wet smoke, drifting down from clouds that were so thin the sun shone through them, lighting everything with a dreamlike sparkle. The new grass twinkled as if every blade was made of glass and anyone who walked on it would break it. The children sat in the house, their chins resting in their hands, and stared out at the garden.

By the open french windows the children's grandfather, back from a life at sea, sat on a kitchen chair and smoked his pipe. The day was so peaceful that even the bees buzzed silently. Everyone felt themselves being lulled to sleep.

Through the open window came the wonderful smell of soft new rain on warm grass. It was that lush smell that first comes to you in your childhood and sits quietly in the back of your brain until you die. And for the rest of your life, every time it returns, it brings with it the same magic drawn up from the roots of the earth. It is the same smell that our most ancient ancestors, long before they walked on two legs and were human, caught in the mosses and ferns of the primeval swamps. It goes back far longer than that and tells you so by the shiver it sends down your spine. Its caressing softness filtered into the children's senses, marking them for ever, labelling them as two more specks in the palm of nature's hand.

Sunshine replaced the rain and the swallows came back from Africa. In great sweeping waves they flew across Spain and north over France. They swept across the sea and spread out along the south coast of England on the journey back to their old homes. As they moved northwards they split up into smaller and smaller groups. Last year's children followed their parents back to the nests where they had been born. Under bridges, in dark caves, in the roofs of barns and houses, wherever they had grown up, they made their new homes. They swooped low over water, shaking off the last of the desert dust they had carried all the way from Africa.

Many years before, the old grandfather's sister had lived in the house with her old dog. When the dog had died she had moved away to live by the sea and for many years the house had stood sad and empty. Like the hibernating animals waiting for summer, so the house had waited for life to return to its rooms. Only Ethel, the old chicken, had been left behind. Only she had still been there when the old lady's nephew brought his family to live in the house. Now Ethel was gone too, but life never sleeps and Ethel's children still scratched and fussed about the garden. The old dog was buried beneath his favourite tree, and on hot summer days that was where Rosie took shelter from the midday sun.

The years passed, the grandfather went to live by the sea and the children grew up and moved away. Rosie's beard turned from brown to grey and Ethel's children had children of their own.

And through it all the old house and its wild and wonderful garden grew older and older, and as each year passed and each new coat of paint was added, generation after generation of children and animals made the house called fourteen their home.

SID THE MOSQUITO

Colin Thompson

It had been no fun wiggling around in the pond as a larva and the only thing that had kept Sid going had been the thought of biting a nice soft human leg.

Sid the Mosquito isn't the only one exploring the delights of an abandoned house and overgrown garden.

Derek the Rat is sniffing out old socks for supper.

Ethel the Chicken is busy trying to persuade the world that she is NOT an orange.

While down by the pond, one angry mosquito is thirsting for blood . . .

ATTILA THE BLUEBOTTLE

Colin Thompson

Flies don't live long enough to sit and think about things too much. They never have to think about money or clean shoes. Life for flies is very simple.

For **Attila the Bluebottle** and the rest of the garden creatures life *was* very simple, until human beings started moving back into the empty house.

Ethel the Chicken is trying to hatch golf balls.

Arnold the Mouse is spending more time *in* the mouse trap than out.

While over in the dustbin, an inquisitive bluebottle is in for a nasty surprise . . .

ORDER FORM

0 340 59290 7   SID THE MOSQUITO   £3.50 ☐
Colin Thompson

0 340 61995 3   ATTILA THE BLUEBOTTLE   £3.50 ☐
Colin Thompson

- -

All Hodder Children's books are available at your local bookshop or newsagent, or can be ordered direct from the publisher. Just tick the titles you want and fill in the form below. Prices and availability subject to change without notice.

Hodder Children's Books, Cash Sales Department, Bookpoint, 39 Milton Park, Abingdon. OXON, OX14 4TD, UK. If you have a credit card you may order by telephone – 01235 831700.

Please enclose a cheque or postal order made payable to Bookpoint Ltd to the value of the cover price and allow the following for postage and packing:
UK & BFPO: £1.00 for the first book, 50p for the second book and 30p for each additional book ordered up to a maximum charge of £3.00.
OVERSEAS & EIRE: £2.00 for the first book, £1.00 for the second book and 50p for each additional book.

Name ....

Address ....

....

....

If you would prefer to pay by credit card, please complete:
Please debit my Visa/Access/Diner's Card/American Express (delete as applicable) card no:

Signature ....

Expiry Date ....